Don't
wake
me

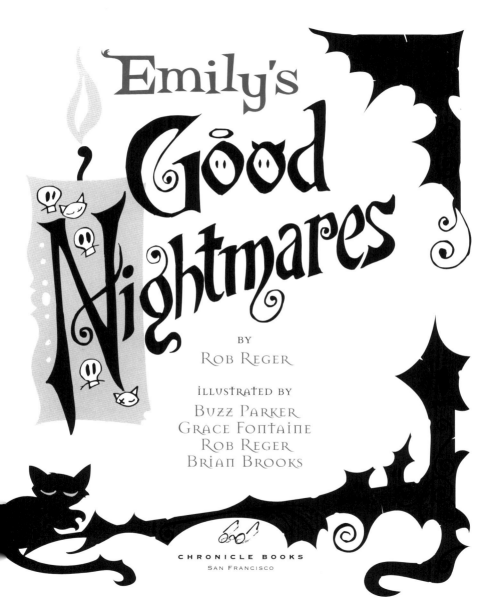

Emily's Good Nightmares

BY
ROB REGER

ILLUSTRATED BY
BUZZ PARKER
GRACE FONTAINE
ROB REGER
BRIAN BROOKS

CHRONICLE BOOKS
SAN FRANCISCO

Illustrated for Cosmic Debris by:

Buzz Parker (2, 4, 5–8, 10)
Rob Reger (1–13)
Grace Fontaine (1, 3, 5, 7–13) and
Brian Brooks (11)
Design by Rob Reger and Pillowgoat
"In Your Dreams" endsheet painting by Rob Reger

COSMIC**DEBRIS**

Special Thanks to Noel Tolentino, Kerry Colburn, Mikyla Bruder, Captain Sensible,
Buffy Visick, the Cosmic Crew, and Lupa the Punk Rock Kitty.
Thanks to you Stranger!

Dedicated to Emily Vanian

www.EmilyStrange.com—visit if you dare!

Library of Congress Cataloging in Publication Data available.

ISBN 0-8118-4771-3
Manufactured in China
Distributed in Canada by Raincoast Books
9050 Shaughnessy Street
Vancouver, British Columbia V6P 6E5

13 12 11 10 9 8 7 6 5 4 3 2 1

Chronicle Books LLC
85 Second Street
San Francisco, California 94105
www.chroniclebooks.com

Emily's 13 Good Nightmares

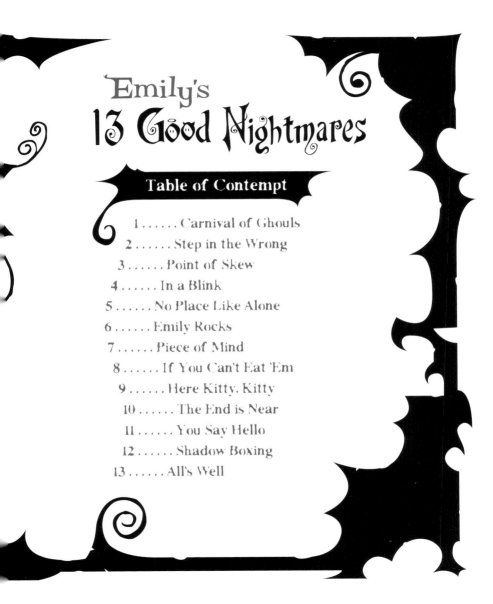

Table of Contempt

...freak out.

A step in the
wrong direction...

...is the right way
to get lost.

Purrspective depends on...

...your point of skew.

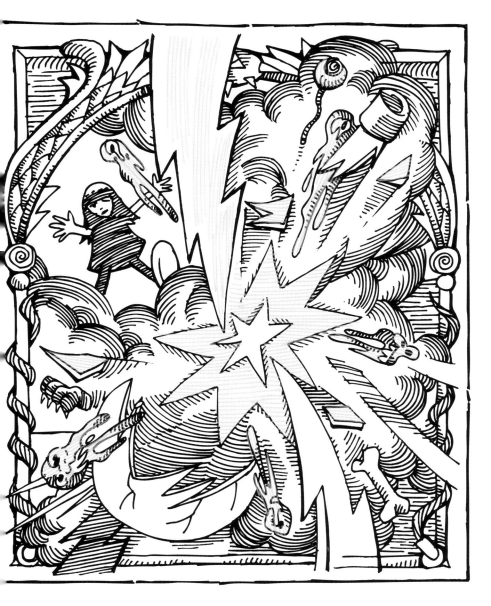

...all was pink.

5

There's no place

like alone...

...unless you have
an evil twin.

13

Emily searches for...

...a Piece of Mind.

1 gray matters
2 prone to sticky situations
3 E.S.P./S.O.S. language decoder
4 gears from the tree of afterlife
5 ball bearing glide connection
6 sabertooth incisor overbite
7 diamond in the rough attitude
8 black light for dark ideas
9 detention extentions
10 eightball powered
11 land of the lost
12 speak strange
13 hear strange
14 see strange
15 time capsule
16 fried wires
17 gone batty
18 loose screw
19 loose nut

20 8 track mind
21 whiplash bushing
22 water on the brain
23 keyhole to the city
24 snake charming personality
25 ESP enhancer
26 GPS scrambler
27 reel to real memory
28 canyons of the mind
29 screw you attitude
30 back of my mind
31 funny bones
32 inner zonster
33 mystery box
34 mind's eye

35 pillowgoat
36 brain teaser
37 feline groovy stylus
38 secrets EmilyStrange.com
39 annoying song filter
40 101 bad thoughts
41 hidden treasure
42 lost thoughts

If you can't eat 'em...

Here kitty, kitty...

...kitty, kitty
kitty, kitty, kitty...

You say hello…

When your shadow
starts a fight...

...turn out
the light.

...that never ends.

I'm
only
sleeping.